Act:
Of
Time

Joshua Terrell

 www.trafford.com

North America & international
toll-free: 1 888 232 4444 (USA & Canada)
phone: 250 383 6864 ♦ fax: 812 355 4082

LIKE A HOLE IN YOUR HEAD

Man, I have had such thoughts
And wish I could get back to them:

One thought to remember
Just one I believe

One time I wonder
In that moment of time

If only I could decide
On which I'd like to guess,

But they're gone now.
Painlessly, quietly,
Out of one consciousness
To a shallow place,

Like the ground,
A pool, or sinkhole
That's round
Like a circle
And accepts all the tourists
But gets them lost

It cracks like a nut
Then slams shut
And bursts.

It is a hole on a mountain
Cracked into the rock,
Where all the pools are going
Down
Into the earth,

A place near to the bottom,
Hollow yet full.

ACT OF TIME

I've tasted bitterness
and kept some for myself,
Stored it away.
I covet it like honey.

To this day,
It clings to my body;
I cannot rub it away,
Nor sleep it off,
Or scrub it in the drain.

I need time.
For when the time comes
The torch will light the muck in me green

It is this message:
Too late, too late.

It is almost time,
Little time,
A penny's worth,
Wasted on suckers and the Breath of Spring,
Or that river's breath
Carrying old smog away.

A slide of similar things,
twisted,
Like an eel in a moat that'll be dry someday,
Or this world at its peak of decay.

Joshua Terrell

The friction felt
Throughout the seasons
Plays no role
In time's lengthy schedule.

With each old thread there comes a mystery

Travelling quietly by

With

The tide

CHURCH OF THE RED-GREEN

It's that green and red
Wood that stands alone
In a group of loners
Shaking the leaves
On the surface,
Down, Down,
To the surface

Of the water reflecting the wind
And wintry sea

Insipid breath,
Unspoken depth,
And the boughs
Going long by inverted fins
In a sea of hollow green
And shallow light

A musky cemented flavor,
Down,
In the wavy dark.

NEWPORT STORY

Asleep at the first stoplight,
Baptist delight.
You knew all your neighbors.
Ponds of sapphire in moon light,
Fish and duck,
Very small law,
Outrun and gun.
Almost like Maybury
Or used to be
Downtown.

OCTOBER LAND

Dead tree limbs
Hide under a mailbox

A great crow caws
From power line to precipice

Traffic noise travels the multitude
Of serpentine hills.

Light covers half the length
From
The humming machine near the steps
To the mountain and
Crisp fir leaves in the chill,

White satellites
Attend the long shadow,
As
I stand in a luscious glade.

And up above,
The endless ceiling
Lifts a tremendous, gentle hand.
Gusting wind and weather,
Sunlight in heather,
Green lights and there they go
Towards it and the moon.

SIMPLICITY

Coffee
Before sex.

Little figurines
With guns.

A chaperone
With breasts

To complete
The picture.

A TOAST TO THE ERROR OF OUR WAY

In the past I've seen live men
   In the present I've seen the deaths of many
    In the future I see only dead men

Like the wind that pushes the mill

For the seasons that sprung
For the nightmares young

And the goodness that dies roughly,
Nuclear tides that wash over us

Are timeless keys in a trench of terror
But will glide swiftly
By the error of our ways.

DON'T STOP THAT CLOCK

What's it like to hear the wolves' howl
And see the starlight one last time?

Not good, I'm sure
You should have stayed in.

When the clock is ticking
And it's going to stop soon

I've no advice for you.

EARTH ROCK

Blue skies, skyrockets, all the trees,
Flying dreams; are we ever going home,
Not this bird's world; for, where will it take us,
This great fortress shutting down
As we near the pull of a star?

Teleportation and rapid eyes
Won't come along in time
For the big red giant,
Just flying in a circle like
All the birds in their cycles.
Bats in their night swarms,
And all the pests.

Not so unlike the man's world,
It's round like this one, but exists
On an actual physical plain,
Sitting motionless upon
A monumental pivot.

War is fought on stones
Along a colorless desert cosmos,
As men scale their world beast
Marching along a bridge that
Connects them all on equal ground
Without shadows thrown down or fear of darkness,
Or time to rest or wonder,
Just a salty stillness that lingers.

GLASS BIRD'S HAT

Tiny clothespins in a line

Pretty bird -

Put you in my *case*

Little black bird,
I see you in the bush,
Covered in snow,

Before it fell
A crispy cinnamon sky
With an escort of
Dancing bluesy weather.

Old Man Crow
Sits on electric lines,
Caws at the dog
Then -
Floury white
And turned to smoke.

Gonna be a red eve, Mr. Red sun.
I see you comin' for pretty bird's crimson coat.
But he can't tell when his hat is on.

Chickadee,

Chickadee, my friend.

HIGH HOPES

A beautiful finish
That women see,
And men just walk
All over,

A toe sustained
In a table of water,
Tapping
Into deeper places.

Keys on a keyboard
Waiting for a tune,

An audience
Waiting for amusement,

Love,
Crashing
In a sweat,

A psycho
Seeking foul play.

BIRTHDAY SMOKE

Sniff that smoke
Burning on your birthday,
Lighting up those pesky moths.

Feel that slap on the back
It was your candle after all,
You worthless bum.

In your arms all the
Presents.

So many colors
Like seeing your death,

Burnt in the toaster,

Rapt with emotional loss,

Ready whenever.

ASH GOD

The crag sends
Circles in smoke,
Mists of heaven,
Over the village.

Ash of angels
Cursing long faces
On the road drawn in
Where the lava rolls.

Blasts of black
And sizzling stone
Flying out a hot mouth
To their ready cheeks
With smoldering snow
In their hair.

At dawn, dusk, and twilight,

They look away

To a sky in siege,

And those rock bridges
Where the waves
Are
Breaking in smoke.

A rumbling under toe
Lingering in the mountain,
Rattling in its cage,

A Demi-God
      Under
        Shroud.

Joshua Terrell

DISTILLATION

Smile Makers
Dream a dream

A rat gone astray
So lean and mean
Like a box of scalene
Triangles

Each point pinioning into musk

That overpowering scent of cement

A slug in the throat

Melts a pot of delightful do's and don'ts

Drowning down in a puddle

Reaching further into the tar

Blackened fingers digging ever so far.

Lean and mean
A smile gone astray
Some guy's Pa who sits alone
Like a stone in the mud

And they will come back to us
In the morning
Like a train wreck skidding into station
Meddling in a way

A reckoning -
Is a pot brewing a bubbling crude
Felt by a wave of ocean water

And

Giving from its depths

One Great Punishment.

THE MEEK AND THE CHAOTIC

Why does man
Cause
The chaos
He needs to solve?

He must always
Fix the broken
When he is in charge

Woman must always
Be second,
For when that day
Comes,

She'll restore to our horror
That unending picnic of
　　　Peace,
By playing
The
Smallest violin
For our benefit.

CAR LEAVES

The leaves are running,
They are moving on, quick.
Oh, why can't we see their legs?
But, look at the cars
All crunched up and cluttered,
So static and eager.
Yet, the leaves run on and
Traffic inches along
Quite like snails on in Jupiter.
If only the leaves could teach us
Or bequeath their mode.

TO CATCH OR CALL

It is the same,
Plain as yesterday -
No more than one way in just one day.

Fall down the stairs,
Take a plane to skyward sound,
Feel the sting of the blade you bought.

Hear the past tunes,
Play the guitar
Enter a parking lot.

Pools of heather melt together -
The strange alien sun dangles
Its fiery arms like eels of mercury.

Like a stranger in a new town
Undergoing some new method of surgery.
Whatever happens, remember -
The clock is always ticking for someone.

UP TO WHERE?

Feel free to use
Our new elevator

That goes up,
That goes down,

But an elevator
To where?

To the Great upstairs
Out to nowhere,

Perhaps a floor of
Big furry bears,

Or a rug that's bare
Of that softness
Your feet know well.

DISLODGED DOCK

Can't fix the dock
I watch it float away.
Old dock, withered
Seagulls are your company.

The dock tips,
The gulls fly or float off to some place
That great big eyebrow taking up space in the sea
That receives a combing to brush the sand and wash away.

WHEN THE GAME IS PLAYED

I run down alleyways,

Hide in the corners,

Take leave in boxes, then lick a stamp.

Listen to organs and trumpets

      Devils and angels fighting amongst the living,

          Or chatting by crossroads,

              Dealing out their cards

          Just the way I eat my chili on cold Autumn nights.

DEATH TO COMPROMISE

This country
Falls in on itself,
As people
Piss them selves white,
With fear of those things
Come back to mind

Moving us
Out of the picture
As if one finger
Had the power

While we scrambled.

And
I do mean we,
Not as if I
Could have had no part.

There's stirring to be
Done, yet,
In this great pot.

Digging A New Rabbit Hole

Upscale tourists,
Black Holes rising
Turning in for one more cup
Following
A sad old dream.

I Toss and turn
With a rattling mind
I speak my name into the mud
That lies far beneath the river,
So as to purposefully lose it forever.

Beach holes in the night
Will claim any tiny victim.

Intermixed colors of white, night, gray
Reach out to the moon with crabby claws.

Crabs finding treasures
Scuttle in the surf
Like shadows in the sand.

What is it like to reach inside,
Feel the earth shaking,

To peer down a hole where
Machines are at work

Digging ever deeper
Ripping away the crust?

Temperature lowers significantly
As I dig deeper ripping soil and rock
Away from sun and stars

And then there are
Those come along to tell you goodbye

My hands on the handle
Shoveling towards the big, big furnace
Then
Downward scraping
On freezing rocks,
My eyes are frozen
Then melt away.

A NORMAL DAY

I witnessed a man walking with his head low.

Another man went towards him and they bumped.

And then he beat him.

I watched as this went on, I being the only one around.

When it was all over I announced the winner.

And then I beat him.

SPIRITUAL WAR AMONGST THE DECREPIT

The Angel is afraid to leave its room;
For the demons will come in the night.
To outnumber-

Rattle their heavy chains
While the little boy dreams horrid,
Of sandy brows on the beach -
All the days before it gone
Right as they come along

To

Affect this haunted race.
They wrap their chains about the child
To placate his ego and then?

The bed,

It moves,

Contorting,

Elevated high above.

Tears on an eyelash,

Tumble down,

As he laughs,

Then steps out the window into cloudless skies.

DEAD ENTERTAINMENT

Pay attention this silence
Before the muddy music.

Rain on the reel
Won't clean my dirty face

The old clock twirls and spoils.
There's a pleasant smile
Waiting
Waiting to open
Open and shut with a grin.

You'll
Dig your grave
Or burrow in first

Apples on one side,
Ashes on the other,
Like a slap on the face,
Halting seeds from spreading.

Weeping people,
Where's your hair dryer?

Screaming people
Awake with a knife,

Chasing through the closet,
Take a sip from Gramma's cup.
Taste that good, hot shit
Stimulate, fumigate,

Tripping through
Enormous doors.

EMPTY SPACE IS A MOANING CHILD

This morning a revolt, a jolt.
Rotting in my guts,
Sorrowful-like
It clings and pinches my spine
Rags and old cloth meander over a chest of drawers
And tea is poured out in great quantities.

The rags are as old as old allows
The smell of good herb has passed
Old men in long T-shirts, old fish in tampered lagoons
Great men and ancient sea worthy eyes.

Those eyes, those ancient eyes
Metal carapace, a mind of metal, and claws to grip
Are sent down the tunnel to scrape raw material

Tunnels escaping into space
Eyes flashing in the dark,
Silver eyes, thousands of them
Twinkling in the starlight

Red-light on my brain,
Only to finally rectify
That briefing in the dark
Twinkle, twinkle
And then we fall apart.

FISHMEN AND WATERFALLS

What were these Men made of Fish?
Was it that they lived amongst these vivid
Streams so long now they grow fins?
I could not say for how they were
Was shown intensely through dance,
A dance of disapproval, of raving hostility.
My visit would give them no more a reason to grant sugar.
Instead of sugar up came water as thin as paper shot of their own, pursed
mouths.

I assured my violence no gratification if it'd dive upon them,
So I proceeded to step from stone to stone, abiding their tantrum,
To huddle below a waterfall.
Hunching down, well hidden, I tried to rest
And dwell on previous days,
Those characters I'd met and dealt,
Like the stories of my ancestors who too strained
Over this quest just as it was for me to continue the line.
My nearest need brought me to unfasten
The whip that tightened, straining my waist.

Ahead of the waterfall, I spied a pile of bones.
Strange, I thought that they'd be just there.

The fish men swam in most brave,
Even enough to surface just below my rocky hideout.
As they advanced some spat but never near enough
Always just short of my hide boots.

I managed a peek closer at the bones,
But while I glanced they began to shake
Giving caution to my stance,
For I had been waiting for this.
None other could break my progress.
Yet, I had prepared myself diligently
And offered the whip its course.

Up arose a snake sculpture, unassuming and even.
Its mouth opened with not a hiss, nothing projected.
The snake was barren of life although fully animate.
At this the whip became straight and answered with full violence.
The snake was no more, scattered, to lay a pile amidst the trickling falls.
Writhing then on the slick stones was a mass of bugs;
I stooped to note their essence frothing from the bones.

Below my feet the stones began crumbling away, and I was just lucky,
For the whip stretched out and gave into the ring on the cavern top
Pulling me to safety, that rocky ledge far from the phantoms of the deep.
Every notch in my cord was now full, so I again felt the stones.
Quickly, I rose through the stair just ahead.

Out in the distant warmth the dry sun cast a noon, which spread
Towards the edges of the mountain but not further than its summit,
Showering me in a gloom that wretched back the light.
The caverns were just now behind me,
And the falling walls of the castle began to rise.

Through the lit mountain, the light passed along the river
Warding me from reaching a higher wall that creased the falls.
Defiantly, the whip branched up to the latches adorning the clefts,
And as it latched I let my feet up to cross with swiftness.
Once I could stand on what seemed like ground, quickly,
The stones crumbled as the others, ushering me higher up
To what then seemed to be safety for that moment.

I was finally pleased. Relief was gracious velvet over my eyes.
I felt the over falls of water on my wrists then let off my boots to soak,
The toes I'd stayed on so long, and I soothed my aching chin.
I would watch the glassy dew wash from the stones I was traversing
Upward and over top each standing statue I'd pass.
One face here a mess, the next glistening and young,
Another headless and without shoulders, a few with wings,
So perplexing that I lost my footing but caught myself.
The whip struggled and seemed to weigh against my direction.
It slipped from my belt to drag along the rocks
Skipping stones along the browning pools.

HOW MUCH I LOVE MY CAT

Think I'll buy my cat a card.

I love my cat;

My cat eats.

See?

My cat eats little candy hearts

That I put in the bowl under its food.

You ought to do that.

It does not know that it eats crunchy candy hearts,

But I do.

I hope my cat doesn't get sick.

MARRIAGE OF MAN AND FEAST

Love brass,
Certs on Halloween,
Scribbled words,
And those letters in wood.

Rolling hills like
   Green whales
      Far off

Not red in a heap, or
     Blue ones in the deep.

People between stone walls
Singing joyfully,
"Down with the temple tax",

Then

     Cringe with delight
With each sinful bite
  That brought
     us all
Here
Together.

JUST A TAP AND A SLIP

When you run through the cemetery
Tap on the tombstones,
And slip from an icy tower
Into a forest cave
Watchin' the red bird.

Don't sit around.

It pays you no mind:

That clock-

Won't buy you no time.

On your way to see the snake
That appears like stepping stones.
Climb them and you'll
Twist and spiral into a night
On carpenter board,

To

      Blue oaks and wide-eyed owls,

Ravens wrapped in red hot towels

    Like fiery women

       And

          Goodbye dolls.

THAT RICH PATH

Perhaps, I stepped off
To stare at the pretty view
Of houses, falls, and other paths,
Destruction in an avalanche,
Wet my mouth in the desert,
Or find cool shade in the sunshine.

But when does one get back,
In the morning or in the night?

Do I remain in the heat
Or move onward from my rock?

Do I find a bush to lay my head
Up in the clouds,
Yawning in the sky,
Gasping for air
In the clear blackness
Of space,

Meandering along a line of stars
Balancing on the edge,

Then plummet

Watching
Them all go away
Up and up, forever and ever.

Would you try
Staring out into
A querying eye,
To be a monotonous blank
In an endless field
Touching the surface
From a fathomless ravine?

But when does one get back?

It is when all the lights evacuate
And that playtime is over
The path eludes you-
Becomes more of a choice
In the scheme of the matter.

INSPIRATION IS INVISIBLE:

I could tell you
I am inspired by living,
Or by life,

Or that complex combination
Of both we hold dear,
Ignoring those difficulties
Pressing us.

And I could say you are
Dear to me,
Or I'm angry most of the time,
And pump stress from my heart.

In other words:

You can't fall from a barn
And laugh the whole way,

You'll wonder just how
You slipped on that walnut.

THAT WARMTH

One death to the next
Poles in the dark
Lifting up a great ceiling
Above a jet black furnace
And that circular shine.

A round, nuclear hot zone
Keeping us warm
Beneath our toes.

That warmth,
That closeness in heat,
Bulbous exposure,
Faithless rock,
Unaware of the peepers
Standing inside orange clefts,
Flashing iridescence
Spewing while turning.

That circular shine
Mammoth hatred from some nameless God
He watches watchers
Sheltered in the deep that fly by
Singing no songs
Only baritone warnings gargling in some stuff,
Like rasping before jabbing up with a trident
Or skewering you on a poker.

There is no bottom
But a pale inner surface underwent with grays,
Shallow colors, no eager attitude or plenty of said things.

A rump and thump in the furnace
Heaving out liquids, no sands in the box
But left for dead,
Above that
Circular shine
From farther below.

THE LITTLE HOUSE

It seemed the day had begun without me.
I entered the world from our porch to
Wind both calm and turbulent colliding.

A dark ring of cloud lit up in the distance,
As thunder murmured, slowly rising,
Then dying far off through the swaying pines.

The bricks ahead at one time were red,
But now appeared old beneath the grass.

Still, the little house sat
Far and impartial while the years had left it,
With a half-double door that swung in the wind.

REMEMBER TO FORGET

Lets begin at the world's round top.
It's a circle down there,
And the jet stream is visible.
There's that blueness too,
A grand oyster-like planet
With all the pearls
Swimming on its surface

Imagine the purest glass to sit upon,
And explore those pearly waves.
It's so clean and clear,
And the air is breathable.

Remember it now,
And take a closer look,
As you slip off the glass.

Relish your home
As you see it going away
Like a crab between a sandy shore
Digging
For what you have never seen:

That night furnace
Twinkling in your eyes
On those warm summer nights,
Just before those true trying moments,
And the spilling of the red sea
Over the edge.

Just recall the world from high above.
Hold it briefly,
For that light up there
Makes it all real,

But deep
down,
In the

center

Forget it all
Know it none
Describe the silence you disturb

With each whispering
breath

That climbs lonely walls

Instilling a calm

Displaying no colors

Inspiring the living to live.

THE FISH AND NOTHING ELSE

The fish,
The grass,
Everything was dancing,
And my Father's pole would greet
A fish,
Set the appointment,
And deliver.

I was not listening
But observing the jerky motions
Drawn by my Father's pole –
Not the line but the fish's lead
Until the dance was done
And its grace all gone.

ONE OF TOO MANY PLACES

There is a house
With a fence as white as foam

A snake lives beneath it,

Beside the pond
A golden thing,
A statue that had once crept away.

The cats lounge in the sunlight basking till
The mist comes,

Dark mist with pearls that blink.
Closely breaching, farther shutting, gasping deeply.

The woods sleep, no animals there wandering,
Only golden statues sidling next to empty ponds.

Joshua Terrell

ONLY THOUGHTS

Outside,

All the gates are shutting.
Shadows of dogs
Bark at peculiar flowers.

That blood eye of incredulity
Opens at me,
As the morning star comes crashing down.

Fire in the woods
Lifting up the ashes
Of an extra, extra long eve,
That madness.

And kind old gentlemen
Handing out square books
With a lock and key
To match…

MOUNTAIN WORK

A man closing his eyes attempts to remain clear
But then next he's ranting and raving from some beer.

Just like those stories of hard men and beaten women
Those children set in stone by their fathers' hard words

Mud, soil, grass that slips under toe

A water table that no one knows-

Showers of rain tide and flood.

Let me see your new coat of many colors
Your dining halls of oak and god-like gold

Slip down to the furnace and feel the heat melt your icy tears;
Feel the breath of a giant before he smacks you.

He is nearing the complete symphonies,
That catastrophic and catatonic whirlwind of noise.

October has passed us bleeding all the way away
The crows haven't left their perches on the cliff
Nor are the power lines scattered for them
As they drop from the skylines, that atmospheric contaminant.

No longer are the dead trees hiding
Or bat's head flying
To trunks of trees,

Joshua Terrell

To moss and slugs,

Trees and trunks of the dead.

To petrified larches and birches that break
Showing their true nature and then Medusa's gaze

Yet, thankfully, none have fallen to the nearest
Limb, face or checkered wood pile-

Where Mr. and Mrs. Snake hibernate forever.

VINES A TWISTING

Perhaps on a night in that coldest light
I nosed on up to the foot of the tower,
With my eyes and feet intact.

The path had darkened
With green simple things,
A garden unkempt, unwanted swamp plants
That stood so high with authority.

From grass to stone to root I walked,
Turning to see, halting to listen,
For those eyes were there,
But where I did not see.

Hoarding aloft some ferns were vines
Who slave till the night is still,
And when that is I know not when
But when I know I'll be dead.

LET'S DRINK TO PASS THE TIME

Routinely look into wine glass

At arm's length
On the table

Drink
And stare
Drink
And stare.

No voices,

Just a sip
To pass the time

Not to jump in the car
And drive off wild.

STONE JAR

Take the stone jar,
Send it away.

I want a race car,
Not a stone jar.

From where was it sent
Some distant star,

Or from some far place,
Or the stone age?

WORKING ON THE TROUBLED

SIDE OF LIFE

Numbers and digits and cinnamon grains-

A cool tide of integers
Smartin' for days.

Like a hot night in Tabasco,
Or a winter night in Chile.

Feel that beaten down earth
And all those working till sun-death

Scrapin' their soles and their souls on cement-

Biding life like hot cola,

Or mystery meat on the grill.

WHAT COMES AFTER

I know now that there is never an end
At the closing of a book.

A company arrives to invite one to discuss
All matters in but a single
Moment in history.

We don't bleed out death
In God's happy eye,
Almost envious for a second experience
On this solid road we travel.

God invented the cheese sandwich
To let us know
He's looking out for us.

"I missed you, old friend,"
To the cheese sandwich,
Which, like us, cannot hear
But does its duty anyway.

When it is gone,
It's still with thee,
Sadness only sore feet.
Able we are not,
Yet continue painfully
As the caboose rolls inward.

And then we are carried
To the other side
When we have grown
Too tired to travel,
That bitterness,
An old rehearsal.

WHO CAN HELP THE WIGGLING MOUSE?

I'm having troubles;
I cannot put a stop to them.

These thoughts....

Come back to mind into my brain-

Turning it into a slaver's house
A refuge for dark, mischievous thoughts.

It is like turning in for one last cup
And then saddled back to the woods
Carrying myself as hostage.

As I arouse the sensations
Of my mind's own collective nature

Those tears collect
This immense sadness

Where the wind goes hollow,
And the howls grow stronger.

WHAT TO GIVE UP

It's getting earlier, almost 6; the sun still dozing,
So what should I give up?
Maybe life, maybe suicide,
The evergreen in the windshield, the rock in the whirly thing
That made all the racket, the whistling upstairs.

The sun-maker slips on a stone every day
To knock my life to sleep.
To blacken every eye with surplus medicine
That gives my chest the pain its full of.
The heart that's loud, it rages and creaks
Like the cabinet I've been scolded for slamming.

Those friends that screwed the cat and beat the Mexican
Kicked in my guts to fuel their summer dreams.
Though he mocks me with a double-chained heckler
Who pinches my spine like the twang of a string,
I wake from the roaring sensation to light of the busy street
Without comfort of knowing a better day.
I'll still feign vigilance to an ugly painting.

Joshua Terrell

THE REAL LIFE CALLED CIRCUS

Some men live
Under signs
Pointing to housing developments.

They would make
Great cavemen, but
Don't give them
Clubs
Till they get in the
Cave.

And the mouse lives
In a tree
Or a hole,
But it has cheese.

A screaming woman
Has to let her hair down
Cause she can't afford a ladder.

The business man
Sees only yellow

And Jasper Johns
Is a thief

Shoelaces are useless
Unless you're in jail.

MAYBE THERE'S GREEN

In the basement they set the sofas in an angle, so in the end the men could be launched over them. The launching was a great form of transportation or a clever way to end the life of a foe. In any event the sofas were mountains, a canyon, or just tons of rock. Sometimes, it was a gigantic sofa. Most of the time, they recovered all the men, but on other occasions, a man would go missing. You should see their faces. Not one of them would go looking. *Just keep to the right of the hole in the corner.* It was just a drainage pipe, nothing special about it, save for the dirty lost toys down its throat. Its presence was disconcerting. For an unknown period, they'd have to share a space with the hole until the spa's eminent arrival and installation, ridding them of ever seeing it again.

That did mean the girls would be spending more time with the boys in the long run. The basement felt wet and musty, not the most correct place to escort a doll, that is, for most of the girls but Shirley. Basements didn't bother her and neither did the hole. To her, the hole was a well her family could work around and her children could drink from. Soon it would just be a hot place to boil her children, and that thought wasn't quite as appealing under the circumstances. Sometimes, a bug would escape the well and trample on her small family. She wanted to burn those bugs in the hot tub. In awhile or more, that wouldn't be possible either. Shirley would have to wait some more before she'd have the chance to boil her babies like little toads.

To the children it was an entity. To Dad it was just another damn thing to do before the party arrived. Sometimes, a deep, watery rhythm rumbled just out of earshot leaving only wonder that ended at dinner. It was to the outside for a bit, but there was always a drain to suck them back in.

There was that old scent that coughed around in the void under the house. And would it be missed? That crusty brown silver edge, was it shinier in other places? Was it slimy? They'd never touched it. Did the men slide on or did they clink and clank in that utter blackness? It sure as hell wasn't any familiar sound like Mom's enormous pot smacking the rough counter top.

The men down there would be sealed away forever like insects. It went through their heads like a bog through the bank in short, stressful amounts. James believed a man lived under the house, and Jessie believed he had a beard that climbed up the hole. Shirley would throw raisins down to him so to keep up his spirits.

After a while, the small area around the hole began to populate with popular items that would enhance the mood. One was a potted plant, some pictures of jungle beasts, and a stale picture of a man and woman rocking in chairs. It really appeared in most eyes like a jungle. This small change lured the children over to the opening one day. Jessie let some poison drop down the hole to feel more comfortable knowing that whatever existed down there might die. James was the eldest so he kept out of the opening activities until he felt sure enough to encourage the situation.

They all gathered round the hole in a dark corner, and James set down his flashlight. The smell wasn't there. They each crouched low and sniffed a lot. The two boys were stupefied,

"What's that smell?"

"It's mud."

"Maybe there's frogs."

"Are the bugs dead?" queried Shirley.

"Give me the flashlight", ordered James.

Shirley reached over the hole, and for a brief moment she could see green. James got the flashlight.

"Are there bugs?"

"I can't tell; it just looks wet. Don't put your hand in, stupid."

"Why, they're probably dead. Hey, is the beard down there?"

Shirley stood up against the wall and peered straight down. James wasn't doing a good job, and while he was saying "Shut up, Jessie, if you want to see a beard then don't put your arm out," she could see slight shines and dark greens. Maybe there's moss, she thought.

SCENARIO

It finally happened, Mark had the gift of flight, and no one knew it yet. He started by going up and up, over McDonalds and watched a horse race later, and spit on some tourists; then, he had a heart attack over the Pacific.

Old Mrs. Old Lady was watchin' her younguns toss small stones at the frogs along the ditch while she whittled something fierce. They were throwin', she was whittlin' and whittlin' till she fell out of her chair, dead. Then the two boys changed their targets.

John gave great speeches on birthdays, children's birthdays, until he said "Today is a good day..." before his death. He had a mouthful of cake to chew on in his grave, that sorry bum.

"It's no use, Frank, we're all out of fresh ketchup and cheap soy milk. We're going to starve like our fat neighbors."
"Well, dammit, I'm going to do something", and he did. He starved to death while his wife searched for ketchup at Kroger.

Mr. Two-faced pinched himself a nickel and was caught red-handed by a real thief who shot him up for having so little dough.

Peter was 14 and suicidal.
"Peter, don't let me catch you dying up there after your bedtime. Mr. you'll have to sit in time out if ya do." Peter detonated his weapon.

There was one child who ate and sang and lied and lived to a very old age. The Earth cracked; people were sucked in; God had had it. It was Mike's fault all along, Old Mean Old Man Mike, the liar. "Praise God for smiting thee and making the universe, once again, clean!"

UNINVITED

They seemed to be terrified of something I was hoping, died long ago. Their flippers splashed below in an abundance of shines and grays in that black stuff. Was it water? I kept to stones that lay lower with less round in their bodies. I did not want to slip in an inch less I got thirsty enough to sip from the home of this race, these men made of fish. Did they bury their dead or would there be fish bones at rest near the bottom and below. I hid and tried not to hear them. Above my head were sooty, craggy towers and moss-ridden walls. This place sang no songs. It sloshed about like a flooded prison.

The splashing below broke for a moment, those long bodies getting fainter as they descended. There was no more a melody but a captured note that settled in my mind like fear or a shadow of it.

Up popped a head. I saw flippers then another and another. They were looking at me. I noticed one had surfaced just below my rocky hideout, and did it show an expression? I heard a bubbly sound and felt a sticky stuff lick my face and begin to drip from my lips. That ushered me higher up. I looked again and they were all spitting. Each one shot a stream of water as thin as paper of its own pursed mouth. I was now certain. They were not pleased, so abiding their tantrum I followed the edge of the wall.

I did not wish them harm and did not go for my dagger. Even before I had a chance to think the rocky ledge gave way like crumbling bread causing me to leap. In my mind, I was crossing the dangerous pacific running rampant with sea monsters. I seemed to be flying because I remember their spitting continued higher and higher to get me. It wasn't long before my hands reached a ring of rock from the cavern top. I grasped hold, dangling over an assembly of creatures and then the falling stones reached their target. I was given a small shower.

I pulled very hard to find land and more questions. Where was I now, where had I been, and what had I gotten my hands in? Most importantly, where had my horse wandered, what place of interest took hold so that his reigns be left for me to keep and go searching for days? I still had the reigns as if I hoped to eventually see the horse. I know I'll never trust another one. There was more to my lonely walk than find that animal. I was intrigued. This ugly place found its way into my heart or that ugly part of it, anyway, so that may be I could say, "I was looking for my horse; for whom I would not be parted". I could not be more right in my conscience.

I needed to find some light to dry myself. If anyone wished to know if I were naked, I'd say to them, "Partly, for my clothes were very wet, indeed, and I only had one pair of everything".

I hungered for meat and thirsted for wine. Why could there not be wine in the river and fresh fish on the rocks. I wanted the food of aged women and the comforts of a whore. I felt no promise of that ever happening. I whispered several curses as I sat there naked under God. The wind was cold and my company of rocks had hearts of stone. That night I dreamed I was fighting with a cave that had a mouth with big lips. In the end of it I was swallowed. Until I was clear out of view, I awoke to a busy fire without having knowledge of a better day. Just how long had I been out here?

That morning, I clothed myself and set off for the falls. I could hear them already, a sound I liked. But later that day I knew the sun. I felt meek under those rays like hot iron bars on my back. I hoped for rain. I did note the falls. The sound grew louder tempting my vitality. But what else lived out here besides the few ravens and bats at night, perhaps, wolves prowling under starlight at that dead hour.

BLOOD IN THE CAVE

Moss and slugs near the cave, that blood trail leading me on, the fire in the stables, rats and snakes, and all those dead horses lying down headless. What had become of my afternoon? I had meant to add more to that barn or sell it or burn it, which it did in the end by accident. I dropped my lantern, and the hay flew up in rage. The fire was happy and went to work. My job was done. The horse, by then, had made it to the cave but was it alone, was there something tugging on its face? I had the reigns but not the saddle.

When the barn collapsed, thank God I was out of it staring at a bloody trail. I was concerned about the horse. Who's blood was I following, our assailant I wished, served him right to bleed in the cave with all those strange blind fish biting his feet. I had wondered what purpose they served in there. Maybe they eat enormous crickets. Thought the horse would be fine with those horseshoes. I knew that on the other side of the cave, if one traveled right, would reach a small wooded area with a stream going down a hill till finally shooting over a cliff. There is, away on, a ruin, an ancient old place, very old in fact. No one travels there, as there has never been a reason to.

I never did get through the cave to see it. The light was nearly gone out in the fields. I had my lantern so I crept along through green and dank, moss and slugs, trees and trunks of the dead, like I said. The blood trail ran up into the cave. I saw those great points like tusks and the cave swallowed me up.

But immediately I felt different. The lantern shined brilliantly along the cavern walls and lightly orange tunnels. I did not know which of them to take, and then, as if in answer to my presence, a loud neigh, but I could not follow the sound to save my barn.

I sat on the cavern floor in frustration. I had forgotten something: the trail of blood. I rose to my feet and conducted a search beginning with the fish pools (I'll never eat a blind fish). Another neigh, and in the water on the far side, dark spots. I approached the quiet pools as loud droplets dripped. I needed haste, but it did not come yet, only childhood memories concerning my present location.

I used to hide in here. I had chosen several tunnels for exploration until I met their ends. Naturally, I'd stay clear of the pools, especially those with a shroud of mist that did not move or play in the stone. Then I heard stories that killed my adventures. Bears had lived in these caves and had mysteriously vanished. After that intrusion I had traveled back to the cave and stood near a mist shroud over which I dropped a fine smooth stone. I saw no ripple of water, no splash. It fell, no sound of impacting rock. I ran out of the cave believing I knew what had become of those bears.

But now I had a blood trail to follow. I knew which pools to avoid if possible. I moved with haste and caution in both legs. I kept holding the reigns because who throws away a good saddle?

Behind me, I heard birds calling, but I kept my focus on the trail, that dark blood on the cavernous floor. Each bird bewitched my short motions surrounded by misty pools and not knowing which was full or empty. Outstretched, the lantern gave me poise and a place for my feet. Until I saw it go dim making it harder to see the blood, was it spread in the pool, to which direction, there on the stalagmite, or dripping stalactite? I leaned on a smooth wall, and above my head a large cricket turned its body as if to study.

A TRIP TO THE DUNGEON

Should I continue or not? Perhaps, the horse had bled to death, certainly after this much bleeding and traveling. Had the trail stopped here? That was when I leaned forward hands on my hips. I stared into the mist, and that was my mistake.

Afterward, there were a lot of bruises and one surprisingly brief landing in the dark. My lantern was bashed well beyond use. I had matches. I lit a match and found I was in a sort of cell like in a dungeon. There were iron bars that were old and near defeat. Strange jawbones, strange skulls; then, the match burnt my finger. I noticed some rags and permitted myself to lighting one and using one very odd bone as a handle to wrap around. This room had no ceiling and was full of rot.

The remains of those bodies very peculiar, abnormal as it were. They were fish-like as if some people lived amongst a river for a very long while and developed fins. I stepped out of my cell into a sort of passage. Between the cell and opposing wall was very little space, and at my feet just outside the cell ran a small watery incline.

This entire place reeked of sewage. The incline went to my left down through a separate passage into darkness to which I followed, slowly making my way parallel while overstepping skulls. My foot would occasionally get stuck in what seemed like a sort of residue of something, at that time, I could not identify. I pushed onward relighting more rags to continue my search. *If only I could find some evidence of the outside,* I gambled. My head hurt from the short fall, but I was not weary. I must have been beneath the cave or still in a part of the cave. This area ran under it, and all I had to do was find water. So I stopped and listened. I remembered that just beyond the cave was a waterfall. If I discovered it I'd be below it. It would be rushing over top down into the valley.

I kept moving until I passed through a large hole into a much larger room. There was light! The ceiling was too high to reach but through an opening sunlight was pouring through. The room seemed painted orange in that instance.

The second thing I noticed was all the water circling in the center of the room, fifty meters across was my guess, and stairs descending at the far end from the center. The water was not deep. I wanted to see where it was flowing, down yes, but to what new passage. So I descended the stairs and below, the water was raining down into a new pool. I was confused, baffled, and more curious.

I dipped my finger in to test the solution. It felt oily. I knelt down and inhaled a foul, recoiling odor causing me to step back: like fish oil, or something. What I managed to do next was dive onto the incline and slide towards the opening. I put my feet out in front and hit hard and pushed with equal force. First I heard "CLANG" and then what I wanted to hear, a crumbling crunch.

The wall had given way. I now looked through a misshapen hole to the outside. I could hear a noisy rush of fluid sending mechanical cranks and a squealing. There was a light hum or stifled grunting of like pigs but not. I could see all the water rushing, oily and black, between two sides of neatly arranged stones, some very near the rushing mess.

I felt I had no choice but to climb out of this opening and scale down to the smooth stones. It would at least make for better walking. Finding my way down was not yet difficult. On occasion my foot would slip and miss the right rock, but I managed well and found solid ground. Most importantly, I was out of that repulsive dungeon.

Now I could step up and down each rock just like stairs really.

I sat. I thought. What about? What I didn't know was happening or any event prior to this. I just watched the oil slick, slick on by. In the water, if I may call it that, I saw things because I didn't have the clearest idea what those might be, looked like tufts of bulbous tissue and sticks, and round objects dragging with the current. Then I saw something that put a voice back into my throat, a body, not floating on the surface, but was dragged lifelessly beneath the muck. There were rags and silvery stuff poking about the arms.

I stood and got higher up the rocky stair. I heard this very sharp rambling sound, not even rhythmic, but like music but without a point, more like a moaning. I moved. The body swept over the edge down into a deep cavernous hole where I believed the sound was emanating.

I kept away from the fluids as though I were a trespasser in a madman's sewer. I neared the falls to have a view of a cavernous dome of rock, by itself, where the river of sinew and bone was flowing.

From here, I planted my feet in the most obvious spots, to me, in order to climb down. As I struggled with each hand and foot the rapid muck gushed by my body, bones, heads, faces going on a journey to whatever heaven takes them. There were tusks of the cave only more elephant-like this time to which if I had fallen; which, I did, I would look more like a horseshoe hanging on them than anything.

I ached as I saw below, smooth stones and ugly black liquid, my echoing groans like bouncing dead men, my swinging vision only stifling the panic in my body. I was only a short distance from the falling water, so I managed to hoist into an awkward sitting position facing the rock wall I had scaled. I pushed off enthusiastically with my arms spread like a falling squirrel or a fool, but I felt brave when I accomplished my goal of setting into the rock with only a bump on my forehead.

I waited shortly for courage; then, I continued down till my feet set onto round and jagged stones that had rough points and above me towering rock walls of moss, like of what I spoke of earlier and then what incident followed: silvery shines like breakers rushing under the black surface of fluid, a murmur, now a rhythmic voice gurgling up and out across each sitting stone with a cold, cavernous breath.

I was standing amidst many entities all slimy and gray, and I wasn't yet afraid. What had I to fear from water dwelling people? They were there, and I was only watching them bob and swim in tight circles, maybe four or five of them near the grayish surface, gray with their presence as it washed from their scaly hides.

It was not too early that I began to notice a change in the attitude of these creatures, more distance, less murmuring, more splashing, less control. I moved slowly towards the sharper stones to have my agility readied for a sprint if needed. It did feel like a flooded prison, or a caved in cage of beasts that knew nothing but sorrow or like a timidly escaped want for hidden things. There want for being hidden became my ruse for only a passing glance till their rapid attack.

I remember escaping and being wet. I dried and went my way towards the sound of fresher water with only the reigns of a horse in my belt and the beat of the sun to further my steps.

TRIP TO THE DUNGEON:

FINDING THE WATER SOURCE

A bright night sat with me around a small fire, while my wet clothes baked. I sat naked, pondering in the moonlight, yes naked. Yes, cold. Lonely, no. There was a stone face staring over the cliff edge directly over me, and beyond that face there stood others similar in height but missing heads, some without arms, and one or two had wings. I saw them as I slept; they were like dead fathers and I an only son whom they were not proud of in the least.

That morning my eyes met at a distance slowly associating my feet to the movement of the Earth. I went. Disconcerted yes. I didn't know where I was going only I felt slightly pushed by arms and legs behind me, and sometimes tugged by a strong rope tied around the moon.

It was hot like I said, also I was hungry, thirsty, shaking in my bones. At least I wasn't naked. My clothes were worth more to me than gold. I cherished my pants. I did not turn around and go back home because I could not identify where exactly I'd come from. None of it looked like it should. Besides, I didn't want to go back that way anyway. I knew what awaited me. Soon, I'd find food and more water than I was worth, only now I'm worth much more and have much to say.

Now, I'm comforted by the clinking of coins and winged women, their open arms to me. And before all of this I did meet another oddity doing a hang gliding act about a thick, running stream.

My hide boots touched on mud that barely held together, as if a great mouth were nudging in the space beneath. Then I tripped and fell into the heavy mud. Moments later a splash of water came from above and down onto my head, sliding the mud off my face. I looked up and saw this beast gliding about. It wore thick wings with boney arms curved at the elbow. In its little boney hands it clutched a bowl, now emptied of the water it once held, and it was going back down to the stream for more when I shouted, "No more, thank you, I'll just wash in the stream," and it soaked me a second time. So I jumped into the stream, and it kept on soaking me.

When I remembered how thirsty I was, I drank my fill. Once again, I was quite wet. The creature settled down on the curve of a winged statue and covered its bowl. Then it let out a tremendous yawn and tilted down its beak to sleep.

RAW DRAWBRIDGE

On the outskirts of this old town, there stood an out of use old drawbridge. It was empty of cars. It still had company, and it still worked. It was just a spot of metal dwarfed by a castle-shaped super highway that emptied its load over the great green ocean. That monstrous wall was also a great big slide, home to hundreds of birds, but at the old drawbridge there nested a few souls sharing in decommission. Down there were brown shirts and skirts, baskets of feathers, kissing on the cheek, and motions on the dead road. Someday, a marsh would finally consume this raw wound that served a justifiable end to many. They lived by a code like so many don't, simple to know in your mind but not in your soul kind of stuff:

Cherish the fellowship of others
Or the fellowship you have with others.
Don't let your home become divided.
Welcome visitors, and feel welcome always,
Never misguided, nor misled.
Have your moment,
But share it with friends.
Carry your joy outside
In case no one else has any.
Carry what you have.
Sometimes it's enough.

JOORD

The demon was good at his job. Not in the least was he never adept at quality. He met Linsey on a Monday morning and led her quickly to Hell, to be sure. Where else do demons lead someone? They don't run people on errands.He watched her go in a cry of shock and blood as she elbowed her gun. Mr. McKindley fell asleep one night, had a heart attack, and was dragged to Hell. Rather easy.

"To Hell with them", Joord'd laugh and then a curl of one side of his lip,

"And many so more".

Joord had no friends and stayed in garbage cans. Every now and again he'd see the demon, Racafus and hear about what Jesus would be doing. Racafus snapped his clawed hand,

"Your job is getting worse; you're in great danger, he burped."

"Do not ride any buses or you'll be sorry you did."

Joord did not listen. He was not the listening type, not even to Racafus. He hopped the nearest bus and crashed it killing only one, and that one was dropped through a hole. In that hole was suffering and the might of Hell. Joord sneered,

"Good day to you...".

Joord could appear to those in the holes as old relatives, friends, long gone, suffering parents or even majestic priests. The dead would clamor for attention and listen with parched ears and burnt throats which they could not answer Joord with. Joord would kindly lift one out, by its hand and with a quick jerk, heap the soul into a fiery pile of corpses.

"Out go the lights", he'd say, So that the false light of Hell could blacken and intensify the darkness.

The screams would magnify and keep Hell alive and fiery wet. He poured lava on one man who fell from a building. Actually, he had leaped from that building but his soul never hit the ground. Joord had snatched it up and taken it to Hell to sort out each individual part that made up the said soul. He ate the parts he enjoyed but left the others to cook a bit more. He loved the warmth of city streets and blisteringly hot days in California.

SMOKY APPLE SHORES

Well, it was a day. Like one who's purpose was to keep one snoring beneath an orange sun in an apple orchard. This man did not sleep but muttered to himself about the smoky towers by the shoreline, the waves giving the rocks a rinse quietly away. He looked at the orchard in splendor, "I eat apples today!" he announced to no one. He took three steps, eyes on the ground, stooped over, and picked an apple. Without further inspection, for who needs more took a large bite.

When met by a visitor in an orchard you give nothing but the strongest attention to that one, for behind this man who had on a gray coat and a round brimmed, yet equally gray, hat heard,

"You look healthy eating so many apples."

Old Gray turned to face a man without skin, hair, muscle, and organs.
Its teeth were white.

> "Many so more than I could eat, for I cannot,"
> its voice announced to the open sky.

"And why not?" Gray began.

> "Death in me denies it."

"You don't take lunch." inspected Old Gray.

> "Your lunch is my lurch."

"You don't supper with friends?" again.

> "Your dinner my disease."

"You have no name?"

> "Ask us your name and
> we'll be glad to tell it you."

"If I did ask." which he would not.

For a moment there was silence between them, and the moving shadows of ripened trees settled the sun's eye on Old Gray.

"Do you live around here?" asked Old Gray not really wanting to know.

"Your appetite for speech only shortens.", the vile thing displayed.

"You do inquire right, for I am man."

Old Gray took off his hat and stood humbly preparing himself to get to the point.

"If you are a phantom then be finished and go back to Hell. I will be badgered by you no more."

It extended the boney fingers up,

"Gather at the shore with the rest and see it happen."

And just like that, Old Gray left the orchard. He walked out with the strange figure lurching along behind. The air was salty, and a wind twirled in spaces and shadows. Old Gray sneezed. He needed the walk.

He licked his lips. The skeletal figure was wreathed in colorful robes, dragging over pebbles, skipping stones to the petaled ones loving that peppered air, the apple shade mixing on the road passing along. Again, he licked his lips, on his right a rising grassy hill, and on his left the whispering apple orchard.

Old Gray's lips were dry. The clouds appeared rough though the friction he felt seemed just past the dunes, his mind lingering in the surf, a questionable place he did not question. Murmuring wind, crashing waves, leaves upon leaves, his right on a slant, dragging his feet so slowly for an awkward distance.

Where was his garden? Hiding beneath the sand paper under the sun that never did blind. Strung by the slime of the sea or maybe caught in a net. Sunflowers sneezed in the breeze; his hat blew away. No one seemed to notice. The earth seemed to be smoking.

His feet met the sand, that colorful beach. Night and day seemed but a moment apart. Old Gray's pupils ran along the shoreline dotting the rocks and noting the spray. There were no birds to peck at invisible things, but he believed in them no less. He did not see the ghost crab white in the sand nor the pine snake nesting in tall grass. He looked and looked for birds until reaching the smoke. He began in its direction.

There, he saw many people. They looked friendly. So many faces and every other he recognized. No one spoke. He heard not a voice, no chirping.

"I love a gathering" from behind.

"Recognize them? You know them all."

Old Gray remained. He would not greet them. He just stood and watched.

Old Gray closed both his eyes for a short moment.

Am I missing something?" dropping the apple.

"Where is my hat?"

Rush, then silence, a little more like a sleeper about to wake and scratch a scab of toes upon the shore.

"You'll miss the moment.", it laughed.

"How long do they have?"

Just off the shore, a swirl. Night was through the window aiming at the crowd.

"I don't know them. Why do they stay? They must be deranged."

Like dogs of the sea, shadows rushed upon them swarming like spotlights on strangers. Surmountable waves, one crash, then another and a rush.

Then it was quiet, a peaceful prayer left for the gulls.

WHERE TO BEGIN?

Once in a green forest where little men lived, there was a normal boy and a house with a fence. That's it. Another time, it was bulldozed to the ground. Some more people moved there and thought it rather nice and built a small cottage. Ferocious bears came to live in it, so they paid a little girl to try and talk to those furry beasts. She failed. Jimmy used to go there, and he fell into a ravine. Over a generous and warm period of precious time a family moved to that very spot in the dark woods. They had a boy, but sadly, Mom and Dad fell to a pack of bears, so the boy put up a sign to warn others and decided to stay in the house. Once he set foot inside an old woman put him to work. He sweated like a dog and fed only on dry leaves she hoisted in a bag. He munched and munched, but his appetite only grew for the finer things. Savagely, he beat her to death. Some days were wet, some days were dry, and some had fires. He lived to a certain very specific age.

A VERY GOOD CHAPTER

Upstairs, Dad and Mom were having toast. It was to be another bright and cheery day. The squirrels didn't look quite so angry now, but they should be angry. Squirrels get hit by cars especially on nice days like this where motorists drive around for sport.

Some drive sleek, elegant vehicles that remind one of salad dressing in the right places and to many a speeding death machine that wrecks a fine salad. Others drive big lumbering behemoths full of deadly weapons and bigger mops to mop up the enormous mess.

Mr. Bedsley was going to see his psychiatrist, and on his way he smashed old Mrs. Weatherby, and she cursed him and cursed him over and over till the moon came up beaming happily.

Once upon a time some kids played in a ditch up to their necks with water full of sharp rocks and broken glass. They were well protected in their magic armor they imagined but were really bleeding. While that was happening squirrels rained acorns down on Mr. Bedsley's evil car, children swung from tree limbs landing on their backs, and police sat in their cars giving no notice to the highway robbery going on in the Bakery.

"You need more fiber", said the owner.

"I hate bread, but I have to work somewhere".
"It's the irony of living", said the electrician.

Outside, the post office was closing, and people scrambled for stamps.

"I hate stamps, but I'm paid to lick them".

Away down south an old man spent his afternoon sneezing on a boat, and he never licked a stamp in his life. He had enough sense to remain a hermit.

"For the love of God, Herbert, eat your spinach or you'll be cursed and bald!"
"Repent before you lose that nose, you slob!"

Day became night and everybody got robbed.

That morning it blew over, nothing to be sore about, but old Ralph new better. He wouldn't play happy. Where were the rice cakes he'd been saving? He would like to rob them back.

Glen was about to finish a bag of chips when he had a superb idea. He gave the bag to his father saying,

"Here ya go, Pops, there's a great big one in there for ya. I'm gonna unclog the bathroom sink. It's full of clumped up scraggly hair."

And from the father,

"Who cares, blurted in ancient apathy.

Who's got time to pull hair out? If I had time for that I'd got to work."

Mom was giggling at the TV. The man couldn't find the coat stuck to his behind.

Kevin hated pork and when asked what he would like he said, "PORK", to their astonishment and dismay

"We are all out of pork".

Kevin smiled,

"But I forget, I have no love of pork".

They must have laughed until the moon's sadness sprinkled the afternoon with dark chocolate.

Take Jason for example. He was an above average cop, said stuff to girls, was ok at the xylophone, and sometimes finished a race. People thought he was a genius. It's sad when you know the lying has to stop.

Old Betty Straightneck watched geese in the marsh. She hollered. Hollerin' something misunderstood by the geese that stood on a tree. "What's that, Betty, ya hollerin", from Ed. "Ed. You're more worthless than the scum on a bricklayer's butt. Go out and get a pig", she sweetened. He did. They didn't quit till there was none of it left.

Away further east a dog was sniffing for delicious mail to rip up. A block over, a bike race had escalated into some thorn bushes. Cuts and bruises for them all. Mom made them rake the street leaves.

Summer seemed amiss. Hot dog vendors were emptied and people wanted to race them. They were arrested. News got boring: *PLAYGROUNDS ON STRIKE: nose bleeds amiss.*

Martin was a bully who had enough milk to last him the rest of the year. Little did he know that most of it would curdle, so he dumped it on everyone including babies.

Day became night and everybody got robbed.

That morning it blew over, nothing to be sore about, but old Ralph new better. He wasn't fooled. What happened to his kids? He needed some more kids.

"Daddy, why do unicorns eat kittens on my birthday"?
"What the hell, who's been telling you lies, tell me, Suzie, tell me, NOW!"
"Timmy says that in his sleep."
"I will beat him with my trophy of bronze".
The beating concluded, and everybody went away, some to do business and others to wash underwear, another kind of business, and other business.
Suzie loved trolleys and would not get in one, the little knot head.
"Suzie, you knot head", Suzie's father, "Go paint your brother's room".
Suzie wanted to change her name to Sondra when she got breasts. It just made sense to her. Out in the yard a dog licked itself thoroughly. The pines rose high into the night, and the mist slept at the roots shivering amongst leaves, and a syrup bottle breathed its last sugar bubble. Life seemed different. A lot was going to change, only day by day or when someone said so.

LOST IN THE WISHING ATTIC

"What is the matter?"

"Why does everything look like a door?"

"Even your thoughts?"

"And feelings. They are all doors."

"Have you gone through any?"

"I have been through a few but think I'll stop."

"What about this one?"

"Don't like the edges."

"And this?"

"Can't fit inside."

"Well, what about there?"

"Occupied."

"And here?"

"It's dark."

"Then this!"

"Too bright."

"You're picky"

"And unlucky"

"Such a sourpuss"

"Wouldn't you be also if you slammed your fingers like I have so many times before?"

"*Smashed in a door?*"
"*Tell me more.*"

"I was shut inside once. Turned out to be a very old closet where I had lost a book, an older book than where I stood"

"*What was its name?*"

"But I never found it.

"*Why?*"

"There was no bookshelf, and the door had grown much larger than before."

"*And what did you do?*"

"I sat down and saw a black line at the bottom of a white wall."

"*The attic door.*"

"When I saw it, I felt like a panicky old man."

"*Scrounging for crumbs, in over his head, who'd be kneeling in a candle less dark.*"

"I hold no grudges but feel just the same. One thought sits by me while two or three whirl off and form no solutions.

"*You could not pay for them anyhow.*"

"There are so many doors."

"*And which door would you choose if it were present?*"

"One that opens and keeps on wider and wider, allowing me to gawk at the universe."

"One that sucks you through to just one place that never changes."

"Where time is dead in a place where no man can dig it back up."

"So your home does not grow old nor grown over with the passage of the sun."

"So that a book does not turn to dust"

"Nor a sword to rust"

"A door where I can step in to be alone."

MOREHEAD COAST: THE EYES

The eyes do the traveling down along the Morehead coastline. Where one is going the eyes have already been from the stoplight at the circle all the way west to the isle. At dawn the sandy sea lifts an eyebrow for the current to comb. Those seeking a place to relish are welcome to it. The days are long in the summer, after all.

They melt in the glare of a tired sun, pink and blue houses working extra long, sustaining pleasures near Shackleford, Cape Lookout, and the island that is up in the day and napping in the evening.

Further in, the waves crash into walls of shells flashing and clinking along to the battlements. Still further, a skeleton submerges then a long trip back watching the shoals swallow the rest. Then where does the nurse shark travel? Try and swim with them and they swim far away.

One stares at the cuttle fish. It is long and slick like a tongue, and its teeth are jagged. Its eyes stare north and south. The eyes of a crab dangle when it scuttles to pinch short, ugly kids. The gar sleeps in a still pool or flings its body into the boat.

Many eyes of the coast, no blue in that water, no telling what may be watching.

WINDING THE CLOCK

It was now Christmas Bear's turn in the old sock at the Miller's. Regardless of the cheer surrounding him, it was still a job.

"That tree has had it," he barked.

Soon, he would take leave providing a much needed opening for Christmas Snake. The snake busied himself more ably in decoration management. He'd pluck off a piece and place it where he thought it best, sometimes completely out of sight,

"Some people have absolutely no taste at all," he pointed. He got back into the sock that lay on Papa's chair. Scattered about the floor up to the T.V., a tunnel of paper lay. Christmas Snake poked out his green head,

"Now I believe that's better," his tongue tickling a blue light. "Time to clock out," hissing a sweet melody near the fireplace. Now he'd have to wait for Christmas Salesman. "I've taken enough time, I hope, so I'll just wait."

The clock hands seemed under restraint. "The last thing I'll do," said the snake as he dropped to deeply rattle himself in the paper. He stretched his body rustling through tunneled packaging and creating new avenues as he went. He'd fix that clock. It would be time.
Just over the clock, he dangled, and the next moment by his tongue, he hanged. His green body tugged the minute hand to spinning, and letting go, it remained in an endless cycle causing more creatures to pop in then vanish. The Salesman stayed out of sight hiding ornaments back in the attic while the snake waited.

If, indeed, the snake were found by the mother surely he'd be thrown to the dogs. Next to the snake were many opened boxes and plastic bags filled with sharp, pointy icicles. He narrowed his way searching a bit for good cover. Then he looked up at the tree. He shot towards the nearest paper tunnel and he was beneath many branches. He was well concealed in shadow and then enveloped in trinkets and fir leaves. He found somewhere in the middle and coiled himself to sleep. The moon went away over the house. Morning came and he was gone.

ESSAY: NOW I JUST KNOW

Controversy: At on time, perhaps the turn of the century, people discussed what a tomato is. What are fruits and vegetables, and what the hell is a pumpkin anyway? If you stayed in bed long enough you'd come to your own rich conclusions: seeds, melons, pumpkins on a vine, spaghetti sauce. Sweet dreams would follow of a yodeling idiot on the edge of discovery. I was discussing this with my aunt over dinner, something good, when I noticed a note sent from my brother way down in Morehead. It read,

"You lose U Die!! Or Burn in Hell or whichever comes 1st. (Goodnight) and eat your vegetables."

To me this had a variety of meanings. I speculated and I speculated. The dog out the window looked very sad to me. He needs breakfast and a bone. Police don't arrest cool people as often as they should. I think jail is a state of mind, a criminal's mind. I think I will eat my vegetables and, one moment while I write this down, have a chocolate bar.

There are three kinds of sex - sex with a friend, a girlfriend, and a relative. Actually, there's more than that if you're unhappy with the alternatives. Now, number 8, hoodlums, lets get down to the truth, not good folks. Way down the road there were hoots, as we nicknamed them, hoodling in a building being built. We heard music playing.

"That place has electricity?"

Go to the toilet and think things are going to be different, come out and everybody has grown antlers for the holidays.

I bought a book called Revenge of the Lawn by Richard Brautigan. He's dead, by the way, of course. Everyone is dead right when they could be useful.

I am affected by a book's cover. Honestly, do books need covers? Brautigan is on the cover of his book, a wise decision, I feel. You don't need some witless artist stabbing at all your hard work.

Joshua Terrell

What has cropped up in the past few days? Presents, angry Romans, lowering chicken prices, fancy dinners. A waving hand over a page that's been finished and refinished. "Life could not be any better," he said. That's the truth. Who truly has the audacity to ask for more? The Devil, I think. He got more than he had bargained for, you know. I get the feeling he is mindful of me.

Sarcasm is really helpful in those moments I find I am lost in a sea of guilt and unlimited debt. Most would go to the car and find a good river. How unreasonable. Is earth another word for cage, and is life a caboose, a cheap one, or is it an antique grown over with too much love?

There was love once, I think, don't know about you, but isn't it a carefully knit thing and not too lazy like I am. What is my thesis? Drinking, smoking, and fireworks, perhaps? Fantastically unreasonable lying? Should I ask an idiot, maybe, or the unreliable? So many questions.

The actual notion of approval leaves me wondering just where do people get off approving of anything. Who do they think they are anyway? People, I suppose. It's been explored already.

Right, fruits and vegetables. Fruits have flowers, and vegetables have seeds that develop. I think that's good enough. This will keep going on. BECAUSE. Some people fight till the day they die against something much older than they are.

FEELINGS OF DIVORCE

I have never actually experienced divorce, but I've felt it over a long period of time. It has been like a perpetual state of divorce never going away. It seems just over the hill, and I've fought constantly both for and against it. We fight for divorce so much that we forget what marriage is, so we just fight each other no matter who is for what.

Whenever voices in my head shouted phrases like "he's out of there", or "it's over between them", I would also shout "No, that can't happen; I'll stop it", as if I could prevent it by my words.

Whenever I had a problem and needed to talk with someone, my friends were there to listen. They weren't the best at coping with feelings; just eliminating the need for dealing with them. When I'd have a word against my stepfather or hear one from another, I'd quickly dispute the claim I'd made or anyone else to be fair.

I would say that he was a good man, a good guy, looking out for me, and he means well, or it'll get better. Still, divorce loomed around my family, and perhaps it still does. Divorce is not strictly a legal action, but a feeling as well that darkens every smile and clears the table.

Time seems to pause after all go to bed and never picks up afterward, but we wait for it, and that's what divorce seems to do in all of us. It manages to sit us down with our fists on our chins while we wait for some answer to come down out of mostly cloudy sunlight with no one to guide us.

As divorce hangs over everyone, there no longer exists a husband and wife, just strangers inside dim quietude all for the meeting where nothing gets done; where leaders stop leading and forget their duty.

OPEN BOOK OF CHAIR SWIVELING
Last Spiral of the Open Book of Judges

Depression creeps up

On me

I am in no desert
And in no hell
I just don't feel so well.

It is good at night
When no one can see,

I make believe
And wonder
Woefully.

In a moment
Those tears
Roll back and wait for loneliness
Just when I think it has come.

One torrent,
A hurricane,
A mighty rain,

The floor a flood,
And in my hands, a pond,
And on my shirt, a river runs rampant

Songs of old friends,
Smiles from old ladies,
And a stillness I cannot get by.

My weakness, that mystery death,
All in my stomach
Churning into a soup
That clambers out my mouth
In a wailing weeping wail.

I twist in my chair and

Note the mess on the floor

Then close my eyes,
Chair swivel till I am very dizzy.

As monumental daylight streams in
The window pain without pain,

I, then

Think about all the mistakes and opportunities
Once given -
And then
Flashed on
By gone
And lost
Toward a ghostly end,
My humble friend.

Do wish me luck though,
Not as if I could not part with such a disease
Of disapproval, of judgment without judges.

And not just with them gone
Not merely present company to accept as friends
Not even pleasing to be thoughtful for their opinions.

I leave this line a note to the one who reads it.

My sincerest apologies.
I will continue to amend
This line
That is so frequented by inflamed words
And wisdom a flop by the mantlepiece of praise.

Good Day,

My Best Wishes.